Apple Farmer Annie

Apple Farmer Annie

BY MONICA WELLINGTON

Dutton Children's Books · New York

LIBRARY OF CONGRESS CATALOGING-IN-PUBLICATION DATA

Wellington, Monica.
Apple farmer Annie / by Monica Wellington.—1st ed.   p. cm.
Summary: Annie the apple farmer saves her most beautiful apples
to sell fresh at the farmers' market.
ISBN 0-525-46727-0
[1.Apple growers—Fiction. 2. Apples—Fiction.
3. Farmers' markets—Fiction.] I. Title
PZ7.W4576 Ap 2001   [E]—dc21 00-046203

Published in the United States 2001 by Dutton Children's Books,
a division of Penguin Putnam Books for Young Readers
345 Hudson Street, New York, New York 10014
www.penguinputnam.com

Designed by Susan Livingston
Printed in Hong Kong
3 5 7 9 10 8 6 4

· For ·
Barbara, Jonathan,
Emily, Elizabeth,
and Alexander

Annie is an apple farmer. She has a big orchard of apple trees.

In the fall, she picks
baskets and baskets
of round, ripe apples.

She grows many kinds
of apples. She sorts and
organizes them.

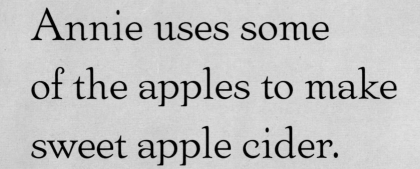

Annie uses some
of the apples to make
sweet apple cider.

She uses others to
make delicious
smooth applesauce.

Applesauce

She loves baking muffins, cakes, and pies with her apples.

But she saves the most beautiful ones of all to sell fresh at the market.

She loads everything
into her truck and
drives to the city.

Annie the apple farmer sets up her stand in the farmers' market.

Annie's APPLES

Dried Apples

Applesauce

McIntosh Apples

APPLE CIDER

APPLE CIDER

Lots of customers come to Annie's stand. She is busy all day long.

By the end of
the day, she has sold
everything. She
packs up to go home.

Annie is tired but happy. It feels so good to have her own apple farm.

My Apple Recipes

Apple Varieties:
Baldwin
Cortland
Delicious
Empire
Granny Smith
Jonathan

Macoun
McIntosh
Northern Spy
Rome Beauty
An apple a day keeps the doctor away.

The BIG APPLE

Applesauce

4 medium apples
1/2 cup water
1/4 cup sugar
  (approximate)
1/2 teaspoon cinnamon

Wash, peel, core, and slice 4 medium apples. Heat apples and 1/2 cup water to boiling, then reduce heat. Cover and cook slowly until tender and soft. Add sugar to taste (about 1/4 cup). Continue cooking until sugar dissolves. For extra flavor, add about 1/2 teaspoon cinnamon. For a finer applesauce, pour the cooked mixture through a strainer or sieve.

Apple Muffins

1/2 cup sugar
1/4 cup butter
1 egg
1 cup milk
2 cups flour
1/2 teaspoon salt
*2 teaspoons baking
  powder*
1 teaspoon cinnamon

1/2 teaspoon allspice
*1/2 teaspoon nutmeg
  (optional)*
*1 1/2 cups peeled,
  chopped apples*

Topping
1/4 cup brown sugar
1 teaspoon cinnamon

Cream together sugar and butter. Add egg and beat well. Stir in milk. In another bowl, combine flour, salt, baking powder, and spices. Add egg mixture to flour mixture and blend until just moistened. (Batter will be lumpy.) Add apples to batter and blend carefully. Fill well-greased muffin tin. Sprinkle with sugar-and-cinnamon topping. Bake at 400 degrees for 20—25 minutes, until golden brown. Makes 1 dozen muffins.

Applesauce Cake

½ cup butter
1 cup sugar
2 eggs
1¼ cups flour
½ teaspoon baking
  soda
½ teaspoon salt

1 teaspoon cinnamon
½ teaspoon nutmeg
  (optional)
½ teaspoon allspice
  (optional)
1 cup applesauce
⅔ cup raisins

Butter Frosting
2 tablespoons softened
  butter
2 cups confectioners'
  sugar
1 teaspoon vanilla extract
3 tablespoons milk

Cream together butter and sugar in a large mixing bowl. Add eggs and beat well. In a separate bowl, sift together flour, baking soda, salt, and spices. Add to creamed mixture alternately with applesauce, beating after each addition and blending well. Stir in raisins. Pour batter into 9-inch greased tube pan. Bake at 375 degrees for 45 minutes or until browned. (Toothpick inserted into cake should come out clean.) Cool, then spread with Butter Frosting.

Cream together butter, sugar, and vanilla extract. Add milk and stir well. The frosting should be smooth and easy to spread.